~~THOUSAND OAKS SCHOOL~~ MEASURE H

LIANG and the MAGIC PAINTBRUSH

by DEMI

Henry Holt and Company / *New York*

To Jesse

Published by Henry Holt and Company, Inc.,
115 West 18th Street, New York, New York 10011.
Published in Canada by Fitzhenry & Whiteside Limited,
195 Allstate Parkway, Markham, Ontario L3R 4T8.

Library of Congress Cataloging-in-Publication Data
Demi   Liang and the magic paintbrush
Summary: A poor boy who longs to paint is given
a magic brush that brings to life whatever he pictures.
[1. Painting—Fiction.   2. Magic—Fiction]
I. Title.   PZ7D3925Li   [E]   80-11351

Henry Holt books are available at special discounts
for bulk purchases for sales promotions, premiums,
fund-raising, or educational use. Special editions
or book excerpts can also be created to specification.

        For details contact:

        Special Sales Director
        Henry Holt and Company, Inc.
        115 West 18th Street
        New York, New York 10011

ISBN 0-8050-0220-0 (hardcover)
10   9   8   7   6
ISBN 0-8050-0801-2 (paperback)
10   9   8   7   6   5   4   3   2

First published in hardcover by Holt, Rinehart and Winston in 1980
First Owlet paperback edition—1988

Printed in the United States of America

Long ago in China, a boy named Liang earned money gathering firewood and cutting reeds. His one wish was to paint. But he could not afford to buy a brush.

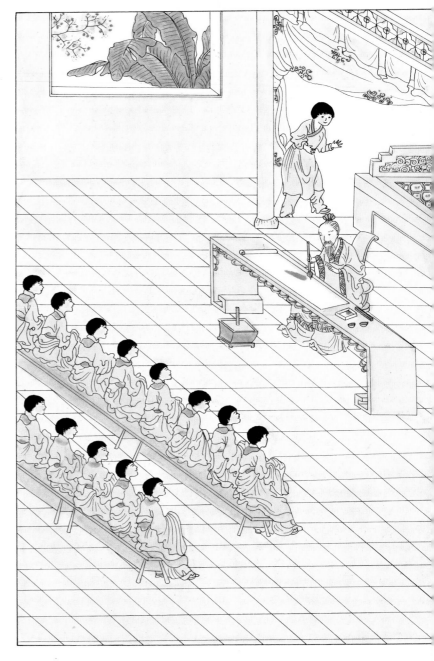

One day he passed an art school and went in. "I want so much to paint," he said. "Please, will you teach me?"

"What!" The teacher glared at him. "A beggar wants to paint?" He drove Liang away.

But Liang could not keep his fingers still. When he went to gather firewood he drew birds in the sand with a twig.

When he went to the river to cut reeds he drew fish on the rocks with drops of water.

One night as he slept an old man appeared on a phoenix and placed a brush in Liang's hand.

"It is a magic paintbrush. Use it carefully," the old man said and flew away.

Liang jumped for joy. "Thank
you so much!" he called after
the old man. Immediately
Liang began to paint.

He painted deer. As he finished,
he saw that the deer came to
life. It really was a magic
paintbrush!

"I will paint things for my poor friends," he thought. And he painted toy birds, horses, lanterns, and balls for the children.

And for their parents, things to
cook with, furniture for the
house, and tools for the field.

Then he went to the market-
place and set up a table among
the other merchants. And
he made pictures of birds to
sell. To make sure the birds
did not come to life, he left
something out.

One day a man asked for a picture of a crane. Liang gave it only one eye. But by accident, one drop of ink fell where the second eye should have been — and the crane flew away.

Now everyone knew about Liang's magic brush. Including the greedy emperor.

He went out with all his soldiers
to take the brush away from
Liang.

But Liang refused to give it up.

The emperor ordered him
bound and brought to the
palace.

There the emperor ordered
Liang to paint a dragon. But
Liang painted a toad instead.
The emperor then ordered
him to paint a phoenix. He
painted a rooster instead.

Furious, the emperor seized
the brush and ordered Liang
imprisoned. The greedy
emperor then sat down to paint
mountains of gold. But they
turned into rocks and rolled
off the table.

The emperor tried again. He painted a large tree. But what do you think happened? It turned into an enormous python which nearly bit the emperor's head off.

Liang knew the brush would lose its magic in the emperor's hands. He thought of a plan. And he sent word to the emperor saying that in exchange for his freedom he would paint whatever the emperor wished. The emperor accepted.

"Paint me the sea," the emperor
ordered. Liang drew a sea.
"Where are the fish?" the
emperor asked.

Liang drew and drew and soon a sea full of fish were swimming about.

"So long as we have a sea," said the emperor, "let us have a boat!" Liang painted a boat, which was soon bobbing about on the water.

Delighted, the emperor
called the royal family to come
and join him on the boat.

"Get us some wind, so we can move," cried the emperor. Happily, Liang painted wind and the boat began to rock. "More wind!" the emperor cried. Liang drew more wind, and more. Soon waves were splashing and crashing over the deck.

"Enough!" the emperor cried.
But Liang would not listen.
He drew so much wind, the
boat keeled over and broke into
a million pieces. The emperor
and the royal family sank to the
bottom of the sea.

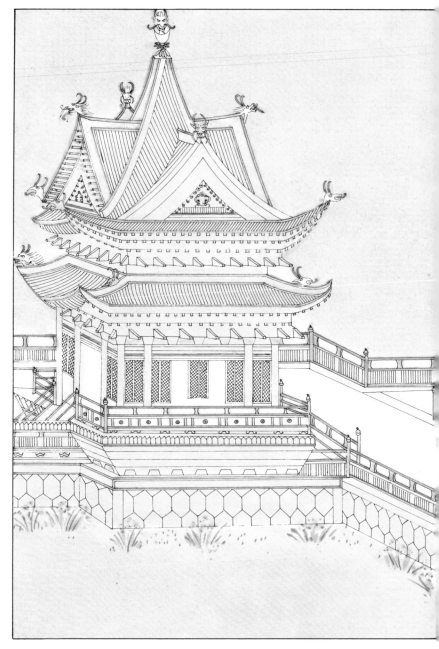

The story of Liang and his
magic paintbrush spread far
and wide. But what became of
Liang? Nobody knows.

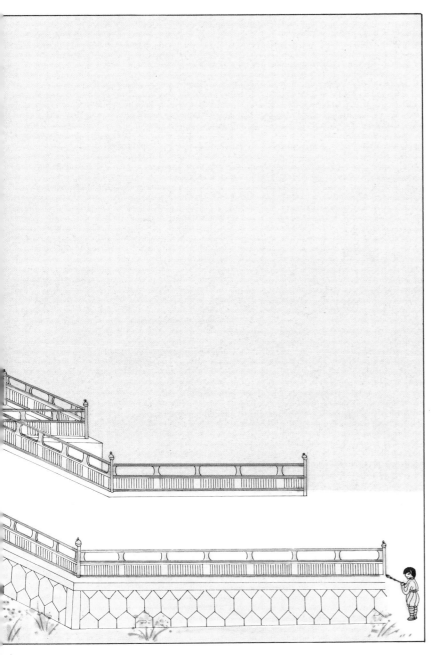

Some say that he went back to
his own village. Others say
that he roamed the earth
painting for the poor wherever
he went.

About the Author

A student of Corita Kent in California, Demi has traveled and studied art throughout the world. She has received several art awards, including a Fulbright Scholarship to study in India, and her diverse range of work has been exhibited from coast to coast and even abroad. Among the mediums she works in are serigraph, watercolor, mobile, collage, and textile design. The author and/or illustrator of numerous well-received children's books and magazine articles, she makes her home in New York City.